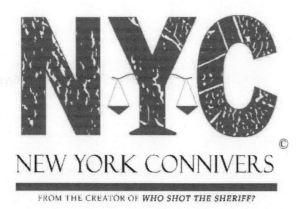

NEW YORK CONNIVERS ©

FROM THE CREATOR OF *WHO SHOT THE SHERIFF?*

International Bestselling Author
John A. Andrews

NEW YORK CITY BLUES
THE UNDERGROUND OPERATION

A L I - Andrews Leadership International
Entertainment Division®
Jon Jef Jam Entertainment®
www.JohnAAndrews.com

Cover Design: John A. Andrews
Cover Graphic Designer: A L I
Edited by:A L I
ISBN: 9798622325243

NEW YORK CITY BLUES

NEW YORK CONNIVERS ©

FROM THE CREATOR OF *WHO SHOT THE SHERIFF?*

THE PREQUELS

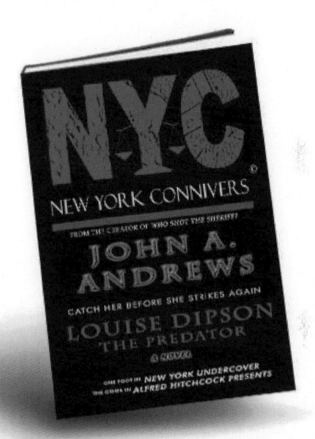

The Pullout

While this literary siege was underway which almost crippled NYC, a Cable TV Station rolled out the following insert:

At 2:35 on the afternoon of October 27, 1904, New York City Mayor George McClellan took the controls on the inaugural run of the city's innovative new rapid transit system: the subway.

While London boasts the world's oldest underground train network (opened in 1863) and Boston built the first subway in the United States in 1897, the New York City subway soon became the largest American system. The first line, operated by the Interborough Rapid Transit Company (IRT), traveled 9.1 miles through 28 stations. Running from City Hall in lower Manhattan to Grand Central Terminal in midtown, and then heading west along 42nd Street to Times Square, the line finished by zipping north, all the way to 145th Street and Broadway in Harlem. On opening day, Mayor McClellan so enjoyed his stint as engineer that he stayed at the controls all the way from City Hall to 103rd Street.

At 7 p.m. that evening, the subway opened to the general public, and more than 100,000 people paid a nickel each to take their first ride under Manhattan. IRT service expanded to the Bronx in 1905, to Brooklyn in 1908 and to Queens in 1915. Since 1968, the subway has been controlled by the Metropolitan Transport Authority (MTA). The system now has 26 lines and 468 stations in operation; the longest line, the 8th Avenue "A" Express train, stretches more than 32 miles, from the northern tip of Manhattan to the far southeast corner of Queens.

Every day, at least 4.5 million passengers take the subway in New York. Except for the PATH train connecting New York with New Jersey and some parts of Chicago's elevated train system, New York's subway is the only rapid transit system in the world that runs 24 hours a day, seven days a week. No matter how crowded or dirty, the subway is one New York City institution few New Yorkers — or tourists — could not do without.

The New York City Subway is a rapid transit system that serves four of the five boroughs of New York City, New York: the Bronx, Brooklyn, Manhattan, and Queens. Its operator is the New York City Transit Authority (NYCTA), which is controlled by the Metropolitan Transportation Authority (MTA) of New York. In 2016, an average of 5.66 million passengers used the system daily, making it the busiest rapid transit system in the United States and the seventh busiest in the world.

The first underground line opened on October 27, 1904, almost 35 years after the opening of the first elevated line in New York City, which became the IRT Ninth Avenue Line. By the time the first subway opened, the lines had been consolidated into two privately owned systems, the Brooklyn Rapid Transit Company (BRT, later Brooklyn–Manhattan Transit Corporation, BMT) and the Interborough Rapid Transit Company (IRT). After 1913, all lines built for the

IRT and most lines for the BRT were built by the city and leased to the companies. The first line of the city-owned and operated Independent Subway System (IND) opened in 1932; this system was intended to compete with the private systems and allow some of the elevated railways to be torn down. However, it was kept within the core of the city because of the low amount of startup capital provided to the municipal Board of Transportation by the state. This required it to be run "at cost", necessitating fares up to double the five-cent fare popular at the time.

Yes. The first subway cost five cents to ride:
Annoyed about the impending fare hike? New Yorkers were pretty pissed when the original subway fare doubled from 5 to 10 cents. Brass tokens were introduced when fares were raised to 15 cents, as they couldn't construct turnstiles that would accept two different coins. Tokens -- once an icon of the NYC subway -- were used for fifty years before the MetroCard was introduced in 2003. There are 60 million tokens left over.
It took almost 10 years to eliminate tokens entirely, and when they were finally discontinued in 2003, the MTA was left with 60 million tokens. After a few calls to the MTA, it seems what happened to them is still largely a mystery.

Back in 1940, the city took over running the previously privately operated systems. Some elevated lines closed immediately while others closed soon after. Integration was slow, but several connections were built between the IND and BMT, which now operate as one division called the B

Division. Since IRT infrastructure is too small for B Division cars, the IRT remains its own division, the A Division.

The NYCTA, a public authority presided over by New York City, was created in 1953 to take over the subway, bus, and streetcar operations from the city. The NYCTA was under the control of the state-level MTA in 1968. Soon after the MTA took control of the subway, New York City entered a fiscal crisis. It closed many elevated subway lines that became too expensive to maintain. Graffiti and crime became common, and equipment and stations fell into decrepit condition. The New York City Subway tried to stay solvent, so it had to make many service cutbacks and defer necessary maintenance projects. In the 1980s an $18 billion financing program for the rehabilitation of the subway began.

The September 11 attacks resulted in service disruptions, particularly on the IRT Broadway–Seventh Avenue Line, which ran directly underneath the World Trade Center. Sections of the tunnel, as well as the Cortlandt Street station, which was directly underneath the Twin Towers, were severely damaged and had to be rebuilt, requiring suspension of service on that line south of Chambers Street. Ten other nearby stations were temporarily closed. By March 2002, seven of those stations had reopened. The rest (except for Cortlandt Street on the IRT Broadway–Seventh Avenue Line) reopened on September 15, 2002, along with service south of Chambers Street.

Since the 2000s, expansions include the 7 Subway Extension that opened in September 2015, and the Second Avenue Subway, the first phase of which opened on January 1, 2017. However, at the same time, under-investment in the subway system led to a transit crisis that peaked in 2017.

Since its opening in 1904, in addition to the effects of Hurricane Sandy in 2014, this is by far the most crippling tragedy imaginarily to ever hit the NYC Subway System. Not only crippling the city but could have long-lasting effects.

TABLE OF CONTENTS

1

Gridlock traffic dominates through midtown Manhattan. At Broadway Avenue and 34th Street, this flowing stream of traffic becomes static. To put it bluntly, it resembles a parking lot. It eases up momentarily. Yellow cabs aggressively pick up the hastened but deposit them shortly thereafter.

They exit disgustingly, slamming taxi doors shut, and opt to trod their distance on foot instead.

Meanwhile frustrated pedestrians vent as law enforcement personnel yellow-tape entrances and exits to the underground commutes.

Underground, passengers are in a trance viewing grayed-out arrivals and departures on-screen-itinerary data.

Confused, they grew flustered as well as impatient with transit officers who have no justifiable answers to their multiple proposed questions.

"Are the trains running? What's causing these delays?"

A yellow-hard-hat-wearing MTA Worker emerges. Pacing back and forth, he and announces via a bull-horn:

"There is no trains service at the moment. Please use alternate forms of transportation."

One confused woman toting two pieces of roller luggage tagged Amtrak, the one-piece has a defective wheel so bad the roller luggage wobbles. She engages the MTA Worker.

"Is the Amtrak Train running?"

'Nothing is in service, Madam. The LIRR, New Jersey Transit, MTA, Path Trains, Amtrak – nothing. You may want to fly if you can get out of this Manhattan traffic." Says that courtesy–masked MTA Worker.

"What happened? I'm heading to my brother's funeral in Washington D.C. It's my last gift to him before he goes deep-six. He loved trains…"

"Like I said. You may want to take the airplane. The trains are experiencing delays. Serious build-ups in the tunnels for more than an hour. Try Southwest Airlines, they go everywhere…Plus, two bags fly free!"

The woman departs, determined to use the elevator. She finds it difunctional – it opens but doesn't close. "It's jammed!"

She remarks, takes the street exit lugging her stuff and forces her way past the NYPD barricades. Police with attack dogs and some with assault rifles pace deterring the woman. One dog pounces and sniffs her luggage as she departs.

Several levels deep, on platforms, as well as waiting areas, additional police dogs prowl.

TV screens ramp up with the Breaking News:

"The New York Subway is shut-down and could last for several hours, possibly longer. Please use alternate forms of transportation."

That on-screen lower-thirds newscast rolls continually, upstaging the network's logo:

New Yorkers have never experienced these kinds of train service interruption since hurricane Sandy. Please use other means of transportation.

At the street level, vehicular traffic remains at a standstill. One hotdog vendor now racking up on sales and running out of ketchup, chili, sour craw and mustard, blurts out:

"It's apparent the Subway is under siege. I hope this is not a terrorist operation or a repeat of 911."

A cop close by hearing the word "terrorist and 911" is nervously alerted. He readies his assault rifle while echoing over his shoulder radio:

"Someone just mentioned September 11th and terrorists, all in the same breath! Has anyone informed Counter Terrorism? The Bomb Squad?"

Consequently, multiple cops become alerted, artillery combative and radio happy.

2

The gridlock builds city-wide, expanding towards the entire Eastside and now impeding the FDR Highway traffic flow. Not only multiple street blocks but multiple train stops in the NYC vicinity have now become an atrocious traffic nightmare. Compounded with cops and their bomb-sniffing dogs.

To say the least this whole thing is a total mess inundated with pedestrians, vehicles, tooting horns and sirens.

At the Grand Central Terminal, the waiting areas have become elbow roomed only with disgruntled unnerved potential passengers. Those giant display screens depicting train arrivals and departures all say canceled. More cursing and swearing erupts from those dissatisfied bombastic commuters. Some displaying one-finger sign to Train Service workers and the Amtrak Police.

For toddlers, it's not a happy traveling experience, evident by several temper tantrum alarms. Their guardians and or parents pacify:

"Hush! Hush! Down by the station early in the morning. See the big puffer trains. They all say no, no! Today we don't go!"

Cooperative toddlers recite it fully after just a few tries. The ones who don't get it show off their snooty noses. Police with their sniffing dogs roam and survey.

Some law enforcement personnel investigate like hawks on steroids. Counter-Terrorism Task Force lettering in milk-white, beams from their jackets.

On the streets, surface transportation relaxes. From the air, the scene looks like the great Manhattan Standstill. MTA buses providing shuttle service to avoid the traffic melee goes nowhere. Streets burst through their seams with pedestrians. Some swearing. Some sucking up. Others, blaming the Mayor for splitting up the street in rural areas and installing bus lanes. Some complaining about that projected fare-hike. Some even blamed the current US President.

On top of the private traffic reduction, these buses equipped with still cameras capture pictures of bus lane violators and the MTA later forwards a citation by mail.

A group of boisterous demonstrators emerge with signs and placards which reads: *Stop the fare-hike. Give workers what's due to them!*

Complainants rant and rave: *The MTA should have kept those dinosaur buses instead of buying the state-of-the-art buses and then increase the fare for ridership. We don't need their Wi-Fi. We have that at home. What we need is for them to stop taking advantage of us.*

3

Underground, back at Broadway Avenue and the lower thirties, a handful of technicians in leftover computer booths huddle as they troubleshoot the underground connection problem. Which seemed to pierce a crater-sized hole in our operations. They are tasked with diagnosing what caused the glitch and try to fix it swiftly.

To them and other NYC authorities, whatever caused this has been and still is anonymous. Instead of the favorite mantra:

"Please stay away from the platform's edge."

It has now been replaced with:

"There is no train service at the moment. Please use shuttle buses upstairs or use alternate forms of transportation until service is restored."

Between Grand Central Terminal and 35th Streets at a subterranean level and inside a similar booth, multiple technicians fiddle with wires diagnosing what may have caused this service glitch.

Tension mounts as two Transit Police Officers claim responsibility for sabotaging the underground operations. At this time, though, their identity remains under wraps. The entire area outside Madison Square Garden is now littered with News Reporters, journalists and all forms of TV, Radio, Newspaper editors and mostly angry pedestrians. "Whodunit" becomes the short prevailing question.

Never before in the history of New York City, has underground train service been so catastrophic. All elevators at Madison Square Garden are a no-go. So, are doors leading up and down stairwells.

"It's an inside job. That's what sources have been reporting. Even so, our network has not yet confirmed this."

Says an eager and overwhelmed reporter at their station's news desk. People in Times Square watch this story unfold on those large mounted TV screen monitors.

On the top floor at MSG, a uniformed NYPD Transit officer Clifton Reid drags a handcuffed elevator serviceman out of an elevator and unites him with three other handcuffed and muzzled hostages. This split-screen video feed also frames the mirrored top floor at Grand Central Terminal.

At this other location, Transit officer Monica Tillerson replicates but on a higher level with three hostages in a corner, one woman and two men. Her gun they can smell and it's Sulphur itches their nostrils. Still enamored with limited information regarding these perpetrators.

On the ground at MSG, The Police Commissioner is on edge, so are multiple MTA officials.

"This is a siege-like non-other."

Says a legal astute gentleman dressed in a suit and tie interviewee with a cable Channel. He draws a crowd while he writes meticulously on his clipboard.

4

On the ground and across the way, the New York Mayor and his entourage arrive. News Reporters dart in his direction extending their microphones in his face.

"Mr. Mayor, how do you access the situation and how soon do you think train service is going to be restored?"

"We've never seen anything like this in the history of New York City. This has outclassed Hurricane Sandy."
"I'm told. The trains are backed up in four Boroughs and also affecting the schedules of the Staten Island Ferry."
Says the reporter.
"Yes. Because there is no train service at Bowling Green Station and neighboring stations, the Staten Island Ferry remains docked in Staten Island. The Brooklyn and Queens tubes leading into Manhattan, I'm told are also clogged with stalled trains. This is not good for our city. However, we are told the train companies are working on it and we hope the service would be restored shortly."
Says the Mayor.
"Some say it's an inside job?"
Says the reporter.
"That has not yet been confirmed."
Says the Mayor.
"We overheard the sabotage was carried out by two transit Police Officers."
States the Reporter.
"Yes. That's what was reported. As I said before, this has not yet been confirmed."
Says the Mayor.
"Mr. Mayor, thanks for talking with us."
Says the Reporter.

"You bet. As soon as we know more, we would be happy to provide an update."

The Mayor turns to leave.

Another News Reporter presses with a microphone extended in the Mayor's face.

"Mr. Mayor, what would you say to the millions of commuters who are stuck in this transportation dilemma? Secondly, are there other accomplices besides those two Transit Police officers who've claimed responsibility?"

Asks this News Reporter.

"Much of that reporting is still speculative as far as we are concerned. To your other question: We are working on restoring service as soon as possible. You asked if there are additional accomplices. This condition is still under investigation. I would advise all train riders to find alternate means of transportation until this situation is resolved."

Says the Mayor.

"Thanks. Mr. Mayor."

Says the Reporter.

"You are welcomed."

Replies, the Mayor.

Outside MSG the perimeter is beleaguered with cops and additional bomb-sniffing dogs. The feed, on those ground floor monitors depicting the siege, grows dark and finally disintegrates. Techies on the ground scurry to reboot and or restore for that lost transmission

5

Inside the NYPD office two Detectives: Jonathan Hobbs, nicknamed "Hans" who assumes everyone owes him a favor and Jamie Johnson, nicknamed "J.J." a skilled street cop becomes informed during a phone call.

"Are they part of a domestic terrorist cell?

Any Bombs?

Who's negotiating?"

"No one knows."

Replies an underling.

Who is behind this? Iran? Al Qaeda? Isis? Syria? China? North Korea? The Russians?"

Asks Hobbs.

"What do they want?

Did they say?

Two locations?

So, we are dealing with split-screen criminal sabotage on the NYC trains systems?"

Jamie Johnson now with the receiver hanging in the air…

"It has been confirmed this is an Inside Job! Two Transit Police Officers. One from the Queens unit and the other from the Brooklyn unit."

States Jamie Johnson.

"What do we have on those two?"

What's the phone number in that control room at MSG?… "

An underling still on the phone delivers…

"Got it!"

Says Hobbs as he writes the number down on a yellow pad. One of his underlings overhears and places the call. And the Grand Central Terminal. Hobbs scribbly writes it down and briskly passes it to his partner Jamie

Johnson. The phone facilitating that first call rings continuously. No one picks up.

Hobbs is furious.

"No answer?"

Asks Johnson.

"It seems the lights are on but no one is at home. Wish that loser will pick up the darn phone."

Says Hobbs.

He continues.

"I'm going to be on location. Will you keep me posted?"

"Locations!'

Yells Johnson.

"I've got MSG. You take GCT."

Says Hobbs.

"Wait! Since when we don't roll together? Is this the new normal? Splitting us up?"

Hobbs is still on the phone.

"It looks like we are going to have to call in hostage negotiators."

He says while staring at Johnson for some support.

"Great. Let's get to those twin-sites before they do."

Says Johnson.

They split up and head out briskly.

Hobbs arrives at MSG via helicopter. NYPD officers surround this new arrival looking for answers.

"Where is the negotiator?"

Asks Hobbs.

"Stuck in traffic."
Says the Officer.
"Where?"
Asks Hobbs.
"Brooklyn Bridge. He is making it on foot."
Says and NYPD officer.
"Foot?"
Asks Hobbs, who, paces – peeved.
Meanwhile, multiple blocks away, Detective Jamie Johnson precedes the Negotiator's arrival at the Grand Central Terminal.

6

With the perimeter of MSG littered with cops, the national guard as well as multiple ranked cops with bomb-sniffing dogs, converge. A TV monitor from inside the ground floor lights up as if by accident transmitting static, and then LIVE footage. In conjunction, revealing inside the top level at MSG several technicians seated and huddled in a corner handcuffed, except for a uniformed elevator operator. Clifton Reid keeps them at bay with a waving pistol.

Meanwhile, police officers are now trying to get to the top floor. However, their ascent is impeded; elevators don't work and stairwell doors are still on lockdown.

Hobbs tries desperately to make connections with the hostage-taker to no avail.

As the morning grows older, the lights in those two NYC hostage holdings locations are still on. Police officers are now trying desperately to get to that top floor setting. Their access remains a non-starter from the ground up.

Police helicopters fly at low altitudes outside both buildings in split-screen fashion and seen on Times Square TV. Nothing much to see though as the morning's fog hinders clarity.

In the meantime, many riders are still stranded as they self-navigate their work commute. Several doctors working at hospitals in Manhattan are bused in and now housed at local hotels in Midtown.

Normally at this time of the morning: places of business in the city are fully operational. Plus, it's the first workday of the week. By this time many New Yorkers were referring to it as Black Monday. Most businesses remain closed, partially open and understaffed. Broadway Avenue and Seventh Avenue are convoluted with pedestrians and yellow cabs, now more than ever.

Fire engines on the run compete for most of the major street's real estate. Compounded with an abundance of law enforcement vehicles pursuing alternate routes. Even so, they are going nowhere fast and like a vacuum they suck up each other's idle fumes. The frustration on the faces of these NYC motorists' looms. Sirens and the sounds of vehicle horns crescendo.

Underground, police surround the entrances and exits at 34th Street and Broadway.

7

In the meanwhile, more information on those two Transit Police Officers drips. Right when optimism over their identity release soared. The monitors once transmitting the footage on the ground level at MSG went dark again.

Techies on the underground realized the computer chip which controls the switches at 34th street revealed vacant slots. It was becoming apparent those two officers who recently claimed responsibility were more involved in the process than what was reported and or believed.

"How the heck did they pull this off?"

Questioned one of those Techies who first discovered the missing computer slots. Throwing both of his hands in the air vividly displayed his frustration.

Simultaneously, the missing computer information was also communicated to the Grand Central Terminal operators. They were appalled.

The only people with access to those underground areas were those technicians, now held hostage. Information soon surfaced: they were abducted and lowered to the top floors of those separated and respective buildings.

At the time the transit police officers pulled this off at Penn Station underneath MSG. Clifton Reid was seen on a tear, disgruntled concerning the MTA. According to one eyewitness: He approached the technicians underground. At gunpoint, he demanded they immediately change the system passwords, reboot the system and remove the computer chips. He instantly confiscated those chips.

He then made a phone call:

"Monica! Let the dogs out fully unleashed!"

Instruct Reid.

It was later understood, his partner in crime Monica Tillerson was located at Grand Central Terminal. She duplicated his efforts at her locale expeditiously.

Reid shuttled his hostages upstairs on an elevator handcuffed. On his way up the door opened and he was surprisingly joined by an Elevator Serviceman.

Reid grabbed him at gunpoint. They arrived at the top floor.

"Kill the power on the elevator! Shut it down. Cease all stairwell traffic."

Said Reid to this Serviceman.

"Sir. The Knicks play the Nets here tomorrow night."

Says the Serviceman.

"Do as I say. Shut them down! Let the Knicks play them at Barclays Center in Brooklyn."

Says Reid.

IT WAS NOT ONLY ADDING UP at the NYPD Bureau but now it was more than law enforcement had bargained for in New York. There, they juggled phone calls after phone calls.

"Two NYC Transit Police officers completely shut the city down. This is real New York City Blues."

Says a tourist wearing a Kansas City baseball cap while clutching to his weekender roller luggage at Penn Station underneath MSG.

People avoiding a head-on got out of his way as he maintained his hustle and swagger going nowhere fast.

8

Technicians kept on digging for answers. With the entire eastside still under gridlock, they sped up their operations to restore train service at Grand Central Terminal to no avail.

"Without that chip and those newly created passwords we are stuck."

echoed one underground technician, who, at one point felt like he was the savior, destined to kickstart the underground connections.

Meanwhile, the hostage negotiator dispatched to GCT links up with the female Transit Police Officer by a private phone and attempts brokering a deal. After asking her what time she wanted, he felt she was demanding way too much. To make matters worse, he articulated her demands with a spokesperson wearing a Metro-North uniform. He, in turn, said her mandate was way over their heads.

"Does she want us to pay everybody? That's ludicrous. If beggars were like horses, we all would ride."

He says grandiloquently.

In the meantime, Monica Tillerson overheard his rhetoric through an unsecured line. Which was accidentally left open and on speaker mode. She felt they were overrated and too Trump-like. To counter she sarcastically said:

"No Deal!"

Thereafter, nothing that negotiator said bore any fruit with the female hostage-taker. To say it mildly, everything arrived dead on arrival. It became evident, they were not inclined to fulfill her wishes. Tillerson wanted it all or nothing.

Back at Madison Square Garden, an NYPD officer approaches Jonathan Hobbs.

"Are you the man in charge?"

"On the ground, I am."

Responds Hobbs.

"We've just received word; the negotiator is still stuck on the Brooklyn Bridge."

Says the Officer.

"Anyone tried reaching the kidnapper?"

Asks Hobbs.

"Sir we tried. The elevators are out of service; lack of power and the exit doors at the stairwells are all locked. Plus, the outside of this building is too slippery to be scaled."

Responds the Officer.

"Who's in charge of security?"

Asks Hobbs.

"Michael Dean, Sir. He called in sick."

Says the Officer.

"Who's next in command?"

Asks Hobbs.

"He's stuck in traffic."

"Who's under him?"

Asks Hobbs.

"We can't find him. He's missing."

Says the Officer.

"Who's the techie for Penn Station?"

Asks Hobbs.

"I am!"

Says an obese character.

Hobbs instructs him.

"I need a line. A secured line. Lock all the other lines down."

Moments later, the Techie gives him the thumbs up.

"Get the hostage-taker on the phone!"

Commands Hobbs.

The Techie briskly hands the phone to Hobbs.

Hobbs nervously looks into the phone at first. All eyes are now focused on him. Nervous at first, he finally gains his poise.

"Are you the Boss? Clifton Reid! My name is Jonathan, Jonathan Hobbs. You can call me Hans. I'm filling in for the negotiator. Not sure I could do as good a job. These guys are very sophisticated but I'll give it a try. I'm not asking for much. But if both of us could come to a common understanding, both of us could come out of this with realized objectives.

Firstly, is everyone okay? Does anyone need food or medical supplies, anything?

Hobbs waits for a response. There's none.

"I wish you would talk back to me, Clifton Reid. This is a two-way street. I'll help you if you help me. You win, I win."

Hobbs continues.

"Once again. This is Hans. Clifton, are you listening? If you can let those technicians you are holding go free, we might be able to kickstart this dilemma."

Still, there's no response from Clifton Reid. Inside that room, Reid sits back eating potato chips and drinking a soda-pop while the hostages wonder what their fate is going to be. They heard the negotiator's demands and saw a cold Clifton Reid refrain from responding.

9

Meanwhile, an NYPD helicopter circles overhead.

"We've got a clean shot. We are ready to discharge."

Says the lead officer on board the aircraft.

"Heck no! Hold your fire!"

Hobbs's response to the officer with an established laser focus. He shows some resilience in refraining but finally does so.

"But this nut decided not to even communicate with you. Why are you wasting your time?"

Says the lead officer on that aircraft.

Hobbs tries once again to connect with Clifton Reid.

"Mr. Reid. What are you asking for?"

Asks Hobbs.

There's silence.

"I trust by your silence you are hearing me and clearly and working with me."

State Hobbs.

"Hans, I can see you now have aerial surveillance targeting me. Are you walking it back? I thought you were a man of your word. You've walked the beat in NYC bullying others. Don't play me! Do not only try to bully and even lie to me. If they make one mistake this whole deal goes awry. I will not hesitate to do what's in my power to grind this out."

Says Reid.

Hobbs now senses scrutiny of his character flaws as a New York Cop deposited on center stage. Never before had Hobbs been attacked in a public setting since he signed up as an NYPD officer and endeavored to earn his stripes. Now to be stripped by an insider?

"Please disregard, Clifton. That's just a law enforcement routine. What do you want? If you need anything let us know, Clifton. Together we can solve this problem."

Says Hobbs.

"The promised pay increases."

Says Reid.

"I can give you that myself. How much? Let's see if we can work this out. If that's what you want, we can call this whole thing off."

States Hobbs.

"Hans. I can tell you are not any good at this. The pay increase for all MTA workers. Which we were promised six months ago. That pay hike! Period!"

"I told you I wasn't good at this. Not sure I have that much in my Chase Bank Account. But I'm sure if you give me some time, I might be able to find some deep pockets. I'm sure the city is well equipped. Plus, you understand this is unrealistic for me to strike a magic wand. While I work on this for you, go ahead and send out technician John Mulroney. Give us something in good faith. There's a song I learned in Sunday school: So just give a little. Get a little..."

"Sorry Hans, I can't do that. I know that song... Mulroney is mine to keep. He is the database for the underground secrets... Amtrak, Metro-North, New Jersey Transit, Path Trains, LIRR. If it runs underground, he's got it. Even the rats! He's inside my back pocket until this deal is etched. Plus, I don't trust you because I'm not feeling you. The MTA, Amtrak,

New Jersey Transit, The NYPD, even our guys, nobody. Nobody on the inside. Forgiveness is like a weapon. It's a strong one. So is justice."

The helicopter once circling above MSG has now aborted its mission and heads in the opposite direction. Hearing all this and sensing the stakes being raised. Other officers look at Hobbs wondering:

What next? It seems like he has this!

"You should have taken that bastard out!"

Says the MTA Spokesperson.

Hobbs isn't moved.

"Clifton, I can see we're working as a team now. That helicopter has just returned to base. Everyone listens to me from the ground up."

Says Hobbs.

In the interim, A Transit Police Officer eavesdrop and buddies up with a stack of photographs depicting Clifton Reid.

Hobbs asks:

"You know Clifton Reid?"

"Yeah. Very well."

Says the Transit Officer.

"Mixed motives? Are you in on this?"

Asks Hobbs.

"Heck no! He lost his home. Foreclosure! That's when he went nuts! Over the edge! Ballistics!"

Says the Transit Officer.

"What kind of person is he? Has he ever been in the military? Iraq, Afghanistan, Syria, Grenada?"
Asks Hobbs.
The Transit Police Officer responds:
"He's not your average warmonger."
"Are they ever average?"
"He's a darn fine officer. A family man. I can't believe he's doing this."
Hobbs returns the stack of photographs. The Transit Officer clutches them and in tears jerking response:
"He's a leader. A good one. He's making the rest of us look bad. Terrible! We didn't sign up for this. It's like we all took an oath to defend New York City against anyone foreign or domestic."

10

On the ground it simmers, as additional information on these two Transit Officers gone rogue pours in. A battle of words erupts volcanically between multiple train service executives mostly juggling for reliability.

"Those two NYPD Transit officers, Clifton Reid and Monica Tillerson... They have no jurisdiction over the New Jersey Transit, Amtrak, The LIRR, Metro-North and the Path Trains. They police the subway trains, not us. They don't even own our computers nor the tracks in our system. Yet, they circumvented and lock us down."

Says the agent for the New Jersey Transit.

"Why did they choose to compromise the underground confidential intel?"

Says a Path Train Representative.

His organization suffering mostly from the underground log-jam as more than eighty-percent of path trains are backed up in the tubes between New York and New Jersey.

"Disrupting the MTA is a felony punishable by up to 20 years. We are already losing millions per day since this entire sabotage began. It's not practical to issue a pay raise at this time. We've recently invested in over 500 brand new Wi-Fi-ready buses citywide. Everybody knows that."

Says the MTA spokesperson while upstaging the Path Train Representative.

"Well, the siege continues..."

Says an NYPD officer a few yards away.

"Let me talk to Clifton Reid. He works for us. Reid owes us. He does."

Says the MTA Spokesperson, approaching Hobbs and demanding the telephone device. Hobbs eyeballs him with a "this is not going to happen" signal.

The MTA Spokesperson is persistent.

"I don't think that is going to work. It could further complicate things. Affecting this negotiating process."

Says Hobbs.

"Ask him if we could meet him halfway. End the siege? Let the hostages go? Remove the siege and we'll make it good. First, beginning with the release of Mulroney. Then we can put the paperwork in cue for a review. That's a lot of money. You can't move a big ship with a drastic turn. You have to make a series of baby steps. This is New York City!"

Says the MTA Spokesperson.

Clifton Reid overhears through his unsecured line and responds.

"No deal. We'll keep it locked down until you deliver, Mr. Epstein. You were more interested in a fare hike. An operation that not only made you filthy rich but brings millions of dollars to this city. Why should we have to wait? Our mortgage doesn't. We have been waiting for... forever! When are you going to stand up and deliver? I'm working on it. That's what you said at our last meeting, remember?"

Sensing leakage in their intel, NYPD personnel moves quickly to disband.

Hobbs wished he had nipped this tremor in the bud. Staying in control was his prerogative. Losing negotiation control to an insider could not only be his downfall but at this moment prove problematic. Letting control slip into the hands of the MTA an insider and subsequently slide to another the antagonist, Reid, could not only sabotage his already fragile negotiations. Fearing, Epstein could not only escalate his war on words but a face-off with his competition as combatant like the use of heavy weaponry.

"What do we have to do with you, Epstein? Just pay your bills so we all can go back to work."

Says the Amtrak Spokesperson in his neatly pressed uniform, determined to turn up the heat.

"The MTA can barely acquire the funding they need for existing fast-track projects and avoid cuts in service. Do you realize what you are offering that nut? What if he took up our offer? That would certainly bankrupt the MTA.

Do you understand: Giving raises to approximately 75,000 employees plus back pay for six months would be like sealing off the underground for a long time if not indefinitely. He squares off at Hobbs and continues:

"That deal you are about to make with Reid is just ludicrous and highly impossible."

That look on Hobbs' face says: *these agents need to chill so I could negotiate effectively with Reid, ending this standoff.*

The Amtrak Spokesperson is resilient and interjects:

"Yes. Even so, Epstein, you now move over 8.6 million passengers per day. Translating to over 2.65 billion rail and bus customers per year.

Don't you realize you are holding up our connections in Albany, Boston, Chicago, Washington DC, San Antonio, New Orleans, Los Angeles, San Francisco, Portland-Oregon, Seattle and other major cities? Why don't you give the man what he wants and end this...?

So, we all can go back to work?"

The MTA spokesperson, Epstein is rattled.

Hobbs radio transmits.

"J.J. talk to me!"

Jamie Johnson is on the phone with Hobbs.

"Hobbs, this is not good. The negotiator pushed for Tillerson's surrender. As a result, she shot and killed those technicians, shot the negotiator and now she's at large. The building is littered with our own as the crime scene is under heavy investigation. As of now, we are not sure how many have been killed or if there are any survivors on that top floor. We are now in pursuit of Tillerson. Got to catch her..."

Their phone connection goes fuzzy and eventually filled with static. Hobbs hangs up and tries redialing. The phone connection does not cooperate.

11

Jamie Johnson finally reconnects on that call with Hobbs.

"Hobbs, can you hear me?"

"This is better. Where is Tillerson now?"

Replies Johnson and continues:

"We're now in pursuit of that bastard. There is no place she can hide. Those hostages at the top of the Grand Central Terminal were grotesquely shot and killed. Now, hauled out of there in body bags. She didn't have to do this! That negotiator she shot from that top floor was the nail in the coffin. He was working with her on a deal. We're now backed up by helicopter. However, none of us have GPS on her. Not as yet. The only clue is the left lane of the Brooklyn Expressway looks desolate. Motorists claimed they saw the runaway black SUV. Either she pushed those motorists out of the way or they accommodatively gave her the right away."

Bang! Bang! The sound of two rounds come in loudly through his alternate radio. Hobbs is rattled.

"Johnson, hold on. It seemed all hell just broke loose on the top floor. I'll have to get back at you."

"What is going on? Were those motorists wrong? Did she show up at your location...?"

Asks Johnson, not hanging onto Hobbs' last words.

"I'll have to get back! Sounds like all hell just broke loose on that top floor."

Hobbs responds and is now occupied, investigating what just transpired at MSG.

ACCORDING TO NEWLY ACQUIRED VIDEO. Before Monica Tillerson abandoned her post on that upper level at GCT. She asked the lead technician for additional passwords to the underground connections. He pleads the fifth. Tillerson pulled out her gun, pointed it at him, released the trigger and debated momentarily. He didn't budge.

"This is the last time I'm going to ask you to comply."
She demanded.

Another technician, a woman, sensing what's about to go down, pleaded on her behalf – staying alive.

"Why are you trying to kill this innocent man? He has aided your cause by handing over the information you demanded. Hasn't he?"
Said the Female Hostage.

'Shut up! Your turn is next."
Said, Tillerson.

"How dare you refuse from giving me what I asked?"
"What else do you want from me, blood?"
Asked the female hostage.

Monica Tillerson pulled the trigger and shot the male technician in the chest.

Blood splattered all over that make-shift holding area. The other two technicians become recipients of his plasma. Tillerson then paced the room. She looked through the window and saw the landing littered with cops, artillery, and their vehicles. Peeved. She indicated to the female technician:

"You are next."
The standoff ensues as she returns some demeaning and threatening looks.

"Do you share those changed passwords, which that fool decided to conceal?"

"That's not my department. Why didn't you get it from him before shooting him? That's amateurish… to shoot first and ask questions later. Don't you think?"

She responds.

"Do you have them?"

Asked Tillerson.

"Yes. I do! So what? Are you going to shoot me if you don't get it?"

She asks.

"No. I'll save you for dessert. I like Junior's cheesecake with strawberries layered on it."

Tillerson then asks the other technician. He trembles like a leaf and points to the recently shot techie. The female techie whimpers feeling her time is coming soon.

"Why don't you ask her?"

He instructs.

She shakes her head "No" still trembling.

"What do you know then?"

Tillerson asked of her.

"Nothing. The desk where you met me is all I handle – HR."

"So, you know exactly who's holding up the promised pay increase?"

"I need that raise also. I think we all do. However, you don't have to put us through this torture and work stoppage."

"That's not what I asked you. I requested the information. Not a lecture on how things ought to be done under my watch."

"To answer your question: It could be multiple individuals. You can start with Epstein. You didn't get it from me. That man could have ties to the Mob. He acts like…"

"So, it's Epps. Sicilian tendencies? What about Amtrak?"

She writes on a piece of paper and hands it over to Tillerson.

"You didn't get that from me."

Tillerson pops the other technician and shoots her too. Subsequently, Monica Tillerson's cell phone beeps. She checks the text message. It reads:

"I'm outside in the back alley. Hurry!"

"Now your long-awaited-turn has come. It's time to kiss your world goodbye."

Says Tillerson as through the window, she pops the negotiator.

Tillerson then opens the window on the opposite end and towards the alley. She lets herself down to the street level using a cord. There's a waiting SUV. She gets in.

12

In the interim, the negotiator finally arrives at MSG via helicopter. Immediately after his deplaning. He squares off with Hobbs demanding his pre-assigned post. Oblivious to Hobbs, this negotiator Randolph Sinclair had been watching the late-breaking news depicting the MSG operation during his helicopter ride to the crime scene. Of course, Hobbs was not willing to give up that prestige. A status he cherished since before he joined the NYPD.

"Who's in charge...? I'm now in charge."

Demands Randolph Sinclair.

"Sorry, you are late. I've got this under control. Plus, I dislike insiders. It's due to an in-man why we are experiencing this NYC shutdown. How are you affiliated with Clifton Reid?"

Hobbs radios back to base.

"I want all the information on Monica Tillerson, let's throw out the net for a big catch.

Find out who she knows!

Who knows her?

Where she hung out!

Bars, nail salons, hair salons, restaurants, spas, gyms, strip clubs, clothiers, antique shops, churches, smoke shops, shooting range, racetracks, supermarkets, book clubs, even the public library.

Her entire circle, kids, first and second cousins, everybody-Tillerson!

We've got to get her.

When you get a lead. Hit me back."

"No problem. I'm on it!"

Says Tillerson.

"I'm with you on this J.J."

Replies Hobbs.

Hobbs immediately refocuses his attention at the clear and present danger under and above his watch – the top floor at MSG.

As if by clicking an evil magic wand, that room at the top of MSG flips to gross darkness. Hobbs imagines the same scenario which was recently reported to him from detective Johnson at Grand Central Terminal.

Other cops and agents on the ground place Hobbs under a microscope; questioning his every move.

Some envy, some daring, and others seem not to care. Additionally, their body language says:

"What now? When does this end?"

Randolph Sinclair departs the scene after realizing he was not a fit inside the jig-saw puzzle.

Suddenly, several cops become animated. Including this NYPD officer, who, before Hobbs could issue additional orders, he radios:

"Lights are off in that room at the summit. He could have killed them all. We should have let the real Negotiator clocked in, and do the job as he knows best. Are you certain that you have a handle on this, Hobbs? Because if you don't and this whole thing goes sour, we could all be dumped inside the trash can like curdled milk. I will not stand in this huddle and let that happen. My dad used to say 'Fish, cut bait or get out of the way!' I know how to execute the art of the deal."

Says the NYPD Officer.

"Go ahead! Call in Ghostbusters…"

Replies Hobbs.

"I can. You don't know who I know in the bureau as well as internal affairs."

That statement doesn't sit well with Hobbs; still finding his way. Challenged, Hobbs gets on his radio and connects with the hostage-taker, Clifton Reid.

"Clifton Reid?"

Hobbs continues:

"This is Hans. Does anyone need medical assistance, food or water? "

"No need to worry about us, Hans. I've got this! However, you are running out of time. Do you wear a watch? If not, every smartphone is equipped with a time-telling App."

Responds Reid.

"If there is an alternate deal to be made, let's make it now."

Says Hobbs.

"The Deal? No substitute. The deal, Hans!"

States Reid.

Hobbs is unnerved by that response. That cantankerous NYPD officer is stapled, catching every word in this two-way pow-wow.

"If you need time to come up with a compromise that's okay. However, in the meantime, I could have someone bring you some food, snacks, and meds. He looks over at the NYPD officer.

"Or I could deliver those to you personally."

Hobbs continued.

"Hans, or should I call you Hobbs instead? You made a deal, man! No need for tinkering with it. We don't have all day. Your word is dripping like water from a basket."

Reminds Clifton Reid.

Now, that same NYPD officer is joined by other cops and agents on the ground with eavesdropping eyes lock in on Hobbs as if they didn't hear what he just declared.

"You are not only putting yourself in harm's way but for us as well. What if when you go up there, he comes down to us unhinged? That man is armed and dangerous. He orchestrated a lockdown of New York City. Why are you appeasing this psychopath? Look at the mess he has thrown around our city."

Says that NYPD officer.

The legal astute notetaker, still personalizing his clipboard now logs the scene in shorthand.

Meanwhile, those challengers on the ground holding their breath waiting for a response from Reid which may turn the tide. His second radio in the next hand transmits and then suddenly disrupts.

"Clifton, the clock is running out."

Says Hobbs.

Reid responds:

"You don't scare me, Hans. I'm no longer a slave to fear...!"

13

During this extended and brewing standoff between the NYPD and hostage-taker Clifton Reid as well as their pursuit of his accomplice Monica Tillerson. The tragedy spun like a sleeping tap in the public milieu. Some claimed:

The Mayor assumed the underground connections could be interrupted for days on end. In so doing multiple shuttle buses were immediately put into play, bringing passengers from Queens across the bridges into Manhattan and doing a roundabout.

The same happened for commuters from Brooklyn as well as from New Jersey.

From Staten Island, the Staten Island Ferry was canned and those commuters were brought across the Verrazano Bridge into Brooklyn and then shuttled across the Brooklyn and Manhattan Bridges into Manhattan via buses.

Assistant professor Marcus Billings of urban planning at New York University and a Transit expert cautioned against pinning down a timeframe for the resumption of NYC train service.

"It's a gamble to put a duration on it."

He said.

"Getting train service up and running again is going to take some time. Even if the hostage-takers surrender. There has to be a cooling-off period before trust is reestablished by commuters and workers alike."

He continued.

Even though some disagreed with him, this was he lane and he wasn't going to be derailed by anyone, not even the Mayor of the largest city on the planet.

Experts from the Metro in Washington and Chicago and even Marta in Atlanta came up with suggestions about the timeframe to getting the system back up and running. Yet, Billings felt they were way off; not understanding the complexity of the New York underground.

A system, proven to be out of tune with the constant grinding of wheels for years. It was a given, that when this system on which the MTA Subway was built and operated on for decades was not built to withstand escalated demands of ridership and speed.

Resulting in constant weekend patchwork to its fabric. Thus, causing excessive re-routings and inconvenience to riders.

According to Mr. Billings:

"When this MTA Subway system was constructed. No one ever thought there would be a need for fast track, Wi-Fi ability, schedule listings and even dominated bus lanes on most city streets.

Compounding it all, ridership has increased tremendously not only by New Yorkers but by tourists as well. Contributing to the wear and tear of the system. That' one reason why this weekend maintenance of the system has proven to be problematic. The upkeep demands are staggering. They are always fixing something. Mainly on weekends.

Most riders end up being shuttled on buses which takes a much longer timeframe getting riders from point "A" to point "B" at a time when they would rather relish a relaxing commute."

On the other hand, some MTA insiders felt these stats an overreach for Mr. Billings.

14

The standoff between hostage taker Clifton Reid and law enforcement maintained a clear and present danger. While his accomplice Monica Tillerson remained at large. Tillerson for over 24 hours like a vacuum has now sucked the air out of the situation and led Law Enforcement on a wild goose chase.

Until now, not too many knew of Monica Tillerson's identity. The news broke regarding her profile in the media overnight not only in the New York Times but on multiple TV channels: Monica Tillerson aka MT grew up in Astoria, Queens. Her dad Ralston Tillerson was a train station clerk with the MTA for more than 30 years. Her mother Candice Haynes – Tillerson, a train engineer for the same tenure met Ralston on the job and tied the knot months later.

Candice worked on just about every train line the MTA facilitated. Her rut was often discussed around the dinner table as she was familiar with every inch of rail those iron train cars encountered.

The passage through the tubes from Brooklyn and Queens and into Manhattan was always of interest to young Monica. She propped up and grinned every time trains became a topic of conversation at the dinner table. For some time, it baffled her how the MTA was able to construct tunnels underground and protect them from water leakage.

The effects of Hurricane Sandy on its infrastructure in 2012 validated her fear as water surged inland and caused a total shutdown of the system. It was then that on Sunday 28, 2012 that the MTA announced at a press conference that all subway, LIRR and Metro-North services were suspended at 7 PM, and bus service two hours later in anticipation of the storm.

Some closures lasting for an extended duration. To Monica, that was an MTA wake-up call. Claiming they had been lax when it came down to designing the underground's infrastructure.

On the other hand, she saw the scenario of trains racing through those underground tubes as giving her the perspective of a spirited individual navigating a challenging life.

Monica Tillerson was never married. Recently, when her name made news as one of the hostage-takers in the subway siege, her son Rick Tillerson had just left for college to become an engineer.

He too, like two generations which proceeded him had an affinity with trains and envisioned after college landing an elite position with the MTA. In his grandmother's will, he inherited her journalized parchment documenting her daily underground trips. Monica Tillerson, additionally, was a passionate advocate for the Springfield, Massecuites Women's Movement.

15

Monica Tillerson saw herself as a born leader. One who created an individual blueprint to get her way in and out of difficult situations. A fan of David Schwartz's writings – *The Magic of Thinking Big*. At an early age, she mastered the art of negotiating. After being a train conductor for five years, she persuaded her boss to her becoming a cop assigned to the MTA. He liked her in that engineering role. Taken aback by her journalizing capabilities. She was quick with a pen and paper.

In defending her decision to become a Transit Police Officer, according to a source close to her:

As the only child, she was not only spoiled rotten by her parents and neighbors but acquired smarts far superior to those kids at her school as well as in her neighborhood.

As a ten-year-old, Monica visited abandoned train tracks, wrecks, and stationery customized train cars, taking notes. Visualizing one day she would drive a runaway train. One which could travel at least 320 MPH. Bringing her vision closer to reality, Monica took a trip to Paris, France. After exploring Paris, she boarded a bullet train to Niche, Cannes, and Grasse in Southern France. Returning to the US, Monica cherished the velocity at which those trains in Europe rolled. It was then she enlisted as an NYC train engineer. Holding down that position for about half a decade.

"I've seen way too many passengers get away with too much. Everything from fare-evasion to vandalism and panhandling."

The source also claimed: Tillerson, if she was in that employ during the tenure when trains and subways were graffitied, those text-free pundits would have faced the consequences. She viewed their actions back then as a total disregard for the property of someone else's.

Tillerson and her partner in crime Clifton Reid worked the subway beat together for years. They were seen frequenting the 1, 2 and 3 trains as well as the 4, 5 and 6. At base camp, they were both known as the constant note-takers.

Tillerson, at the time when she sabotaged the underground-connects along with Reid. It was said she missed multiple payments on her cherished black Chevy Tahoe SUV.

During those hard times, she resorted to hiding her SUV in neighbor's garages, to avoid having it repossessed.

16

Clifton Reid, on the other hand, migrated from Jamaica to New York during the era when Afro hairstyles, bell-bottom pants, and platform shoes dominated. Reid came from a family of two pastors. In school, he was referred to as PK 2.

While at Manchester High, Clifton excelled in soccer as well as cricket. Additionally, he was always the go-to guy when it came down to working out complex problems.

Immigrating to the US he soon thereafter became naturalized. It was then he joined the MTA. Reid began his employ with the MTA as a train conductor and eventually worked his way up to Transit Police. He saw himself not bullying but working aggressively to reach his quotas. He cited viciously, thus enhancing his skill and accelerating swiftly up the chain of leadership in his vocation.

His part-time scholastics included aeronautics at Vaughn College outside La Guardia Airport.

He married Theresa Morgan, who paved the way for his US naturalization. Although born in the Caribbean Island, Jamaica. Reid saw himself as a "Yankee" and fathered two sons and a daughter. His daughter Megan, the apple of his eye and split image of her dad was privileged as the rose between two thorns. She not only knew it but lived it.

Theresa, a registered nurse and a great one, worked extended hours mostly during the graveyard shift at a local Manhattan hospital. Clifton Reid had always spoken extensively as an advocate on human rights.

At the time when Reid embarked on sabotaging the train connection, he had missed multiple payments on his Brooklyn brownstone home and saw it plummet into foreclosure.

Additionally, there was much talk about a pending fare hike by the MTA. This didn't sit well with most of their ridership, including Reid.

On the other hand, the long-awaited pay increase promised by the MTA wagged the dog. Caught up in all this denial, the Reid's found themselves pressured to funding their daughter Megan's initial tuition at Columbia Law School.

17

It wasn't long before FBI agents raided the home of Clifton Reid in Brooklyn. They readily confiscated computers, external hard drives, written journals, thumb drives, audio, and video recordings, cameras as well as other gadgets.

At the time of the raid on that early morning at the crack of dawn. They also took into custody Theresa Reid and their three young adult kids. They claimed these arrests were conducted on suspicion of collaborative criminal sabotage of the underground connections.

Theresa Reid, claimed: neither her nor her kids knew anything about or had anything to do with the hostage situation still underway at Madison Square Garden, an extension of this train lines sabotage. The FBI did not buy into their non-affiliation with the disclosures to the crime. To support their arrests, they told the Reid's: this hostage situation had to be a well thought out process. Possibly lasting more than a full year.

Furthermore, they had no qualms letting Theresa know that if a husband was going to pull off such an ordeal of this magnitude. It was almost impossible for a wife who lived in the same house and possibly slept together in the same bed, not to have seen or heard anything leading up to such a horrendous criminal activity.

The young adult kids also claimed they did not know these going-on which led up to the sabotage of the trains systems.

The FBI didn't buy their story either. To cover their butts, the Bureau placed that entire family under arrest pending their confession or willingness to cough up pertinent information.

During that raid in Brooklyn. Additional FBI agents raided the home on Monica Tillerson in Astoria, Queens. They entered the home in takedown style. Fearing, her, Monica who was still at large might still be residing there and armed.

Unfortunately, and fortunately for them, she wasn't home at the time. However, her son, Rick was. He had a newbie at college. Rick claimed: he knew nothing about his mother's plan to disrupt the trains service. Rick informed them that his mother was a good woman, loved her church and a law-abiding citizen.

The FBI envisioned a completely different story. The fact that she killed three hostages and the negotiator at the GCT kidnapping, and fled was the complete opposite of who he thought his mother was. When asked if he knew of her whereabouts. He said:

"No."

Still, they saw him as an accomplice. They eyed, searched and later towed the black SUV. Inside they discovered blood droplets on the seat linked to one of the hostage's DNA.

Furthermore, Rick's computer's background displayed a photo of the # 7 train which ran from Flushing and into Manhattan. Additionally, his Facebook page was inundated with pictures of antique as well as new trains. "This kid has way too much affiliation..."

Said one of the FBI agents to another.

With Rick already in handcuffs, they confiscated computers, cameras, external hard drives, journals, thumb drives, along with an appointment book detailing Monica's upcoming visits with her neurologist.

18

Outside MSG, NYPD helicopters circle its summit. On the ground, onlookers: some run for cover, some maintain their distance. While others got immersed in the thick of things. Some of the latter display their advocacy towards Clifton Reid. They came out of the closet after the news broke that

Reid was angry with the MTA and documented a laundry list. Headlined: The projected fare hike upstaging a promised raise to its almost 100,000 workers.

Hobbs on the ground, and oblivious to the reasons for Reid's' emerging support, remains in negotiating mode. Yet, after being torn to shreds by Reid's assassination of the detective's character.

"Clifton, are you hearing me?"

Asks Hobbs.

"I am. Hans? I thought you fell asleep at the wheel!"

Responds Clifton Reid, who continues:

"What's going on? I thought we had an agreement. I thought you were going to hold off these flying predators at bay."

"Clifton Reid, like I told you. There's a time constraint. You've not turned over John Mulroney to us. So, it's now out of my hands. Totally out of my control."

"So, you are going to take out these hostages? I mean: have your Ariel squad to shoot them. I could make that very easy for you."

"I'm not saying that's how I want this to go down."

Says Hobbs.

"So, what are you proposing, Hans? Speak now or forever hold your peace!"

Asks Reid.

"What are your grievances, Clifton Reid? Your real grievances?"

Asked Hobbs.

About this time, Reid went mute on Hobbs.

It was also oblivious to Hobbs that Reid had watched the Cable News on iPhone regarding the FBI conducted raids. Now with a few power bars left he elected to conserve the energy. Reid saw during that raid, his items confiscated, along with his three kids arrested and hauled away by the Feds. He remained not a happy camper after watching this occurrence. Anyway, he was able to compartmentalize those raids until now.

With those helicopters still surveilling Reid walked across to that secured phone and dialed Hobbs.

"Hans. You have asked what my grievances were. I thought you would have known by now. However, if you have not already been informed. For your benefit as well as your cronies, let me reiterate. I'll release to you my MTA laundry list as an addendum."

Clifton Reid methodically went through his MTA laundry list. Itemized as if they were prefaced as bulleted points. To him and Monica Tillerson, these were already their documented talking points as written in their confiscated journals.

19

Multiple MTA officials on the ground at MSG were privy to that heated exchange between Hobbs and Reid. They were aware, the MTA which controlled the New York Subway system, LIRR, Metro-North, Bridges, and Lanes on multiple NYC major streets could have done a better-blanketed-job. That potential fare hike although now a point with riders, didn't sit well and cast extended blame on the city.

Even so, they had at the moment a more important task at hand: The mission of restoring the underground connections? This weighed heavily on their minds. Yet, they were not prepared to fulfill promises to their workers. Not at this moment, they were focused on reeling it in rather than doling it out. Tillerson and Reid's demand were DOA.

During a subsequent phone call from Reid to Hobbs. Reid questioned how Hobbs wanted him to deliver John Mulroney.

In the meantime, Reid asked Mulroney to write down all the recreated passwords for those underground connection systems.

"In regards to Mulroney?"

Reid asked Hobbs, with the helicopters still hovering.

Hobbs deliberated silently.

Reid continued:

"Do you want him delivered dead or alive?"

"Clifton, this man has a family. Young kids. They would be happy to see him alive again."

Says Hobbs.

"I have a family too, Hobbs. If you want Mulroney, you are going to have to release my wife and three kids. Set them free. An eye for an eye. A tooth for a tooth."

States Reid.

"Not sure I can make that happen. As you know a move like that is completely out of my control and in the hands of the SDNY and the FBI."

"Hans, you have access to a phone, don't you? Use it! I take it that you have multiple ways of communicating my demands. And while you are at it, add the release Rick Tillerson to your list. He's part and parcel of the deal."

Hobbs, baffled as to Reid's knowledge of external affairs while he's secluded on this top floor, looks for answers.

The Police Commissioner, now nearby and overhearing the conversation, gives a "Yes" nod to Hobbs urging him on.

In the meanwhile, Reid notifies Hobbs through that line of communication:

"Hans, you have only 60 minutes to make this happen."

Hobbs looks at his watch and responds:

"Clifton, this is not accomplished by the waving of a magic wand. We are going to need at least 2 hours."

"You have a full hour. The city wants to see this ordeal ended sooner than later. Doesn't it?"

Demands Reid.

The police commissioner once again gives Hobbs a "Yes" nod.

Hobbs quickly responds:

"Hang in there. I'm working on it! Understand this is a weekend and all city offices are closed."

20

Inside that summit room at MSG, Reid turns the heat up on his hostages. After those two shots rang out earlier Hobbs reintroduced the helicopters to see if those cops on board could get a peep inside that room with aid of their aircraft's floodlights. Tactfully,

Reid had that view sealed off with the cubicles. Nothing to see, the cops backed off.

Moments later after the helicopters retreated, Reid opened the tiny window and tossed out John Mulroney's blood-soaked jacked. Previously, when Reid shot Mulroney in the leg, he used the technician's jacket as a bandage for his leg-wound and soak up the blood which splattered on himself.

That jacket fell on the ground level in that huddle careened with Hobbs, the Police Commissioner and spokespeople for those service affected train lines.

Since those two shots rang out on that top floor, Hobbs has been desperately trying to make contact with Clifton Reid, until that previous conversation with Hobbs went mute. He avoided those negotiating calls. Reid, at that time, felt like he had the upper hand. That floor kept ringing intermittently.

When the jacket landed on the ground. Hobbs took a fact-finding look at it. Not only was it saturated with the blood but bore the embroidered lettering – John Mulroney on its breast pocket.

That NYPD officer, looking over Hobbs' back asked:

"So, he sent you blood-soaked clothing…"

The Amtrak spokesperson intercepts.

"No. He sent us a blood-cloth."

Said Hobbs.

"Reid. That rat. He turned on his department and then put them in a vice."

Said the Police Commissioner.

The helicopters returned for yet another peep into that top floor.

"Reid, this is Hans. We received your little blood-soaked gift. Is everyone safe? Is Mulroney alive? We can send our Medics in to perform needed first-aid."

Meanwhile, cops from one of the helicopters deplane onto the roof looking for access into the building.

Hobbs continues:

"Do you need bandages? Food? Water? Anything?"

"Hans, all of this could have been avoided. You and your guys decided to hang me out to dry. I don't like your games. Don't play me. You have proven you cannot keep your word. Water in a basket."

Bang!

Reid shoots Mulroney in the other leg. The helicopters increase their altitude. Hobbs on the ground hears the gunshot echo.

"Hans, we need a pair of crutches. If you need Mulroney now, you can have him delivered as-is. If you delay on meeting my demands you may need a shovel and body-bag. Have it your way."

The cops gain limited access through the roof now able to overhear Reid's movements. However, the door, seen on the building's blueprint and leading to the floor where Reid is sealed off.

21

In the meanwhile, as Reid continued terrorizing his hostages. The NYPD snipers were constantly working on gaining access through the roof at MSG. Meanwhile, Monica Tillerson was on the run. According to New York's Mayor, when it comes to Tillerson:

"We are fighting an enemy and we don't even know where she is. We need to catch her now!"

In the interim, the FBI released Reid's family from custody. Theresa Reid, her daughter, and two sons were now poised to sleeping in their beds. However, Rick Tillerson the son of Monica Tillerson was still under arrest. No doubt, law enforcement wanted to make sure Monica Tillerson was in custody, either dead or alive before releasing Rick.

The late-breaking news about Reid's family release saturated the airwaves. Inside that hostage room, Clifton Reid used whatever was left of his iPhone's power bar to tune in. He watched the news in speaker-mode away from his huddle.

Above him and still concealed, cops worked tirelessly cutting through that roof. While Reid tuned in to the news and argued with the hostages and communicated with Hans on the ground. Those cops above were eventually able to tap into that room's atmospherics using small tubes.

They were now privy to his next moves as well as Hobbs on the ground. Hobbs, on the other hand, felt by help getting Reid's family out of police custody Reid would be more willing to comply with demands. Even so, that favor did not move the needle toward letting even the injured John Mulroney go.

Associates of Hobbs blamed him. Accusing him of letting himself get conned by Clifton Reid. Some of them even stuck it to him that they would not have initiated any dialog to have Reid's family released. They felt he should have used their release as a bait, hook, and sinker.

As far as Reid was concerned, the release did not include his partner in crime son, Rick Tillerson. Therefore, in his eyes, Hobbs had not done enough. Not fulfilling that segment of the deal.

"A broken link still existed in the chain of demands." Said Reid, who entertained the epiphany, the MTA had not attended to his blanketed demands – dealing with the proposed wage hike. Therefore, purposing in his heart, he was going to dig in, sticking to his guns. Hobbs and Reid engaged in a nefarious debate over the rules of the game.

22

As detective Jamie Johnson and other NYPD officers searched by land, sea, and air looking for Monica Tillerson, through connecting streets in Brooklyn and elsewhere. An Amtrak train, parked at Penn Station rolled out of that establishment.

By the time authorities were alerted it was gaining steam northbound. According to sources, this was the last train to pull into that station, after the underground connections went awry. It was believed at the time it departed Penn Station it was unmanned. One of its doors was partially opened and a manifest yet to be released and verified.

It was also factored into the rollout that the brakes on that train were disabled mechanically. While the speculations surrounding this train's, departure surfaced. The runaway-train was speedily heading northbound towards upward of the Hudson River.

It was soon determined from the air that the engineer at the helm was Monica Tillerson, still clothed in that blood-stained Transit Police Officer's uniform. Multiple helicopters now joined in the aerial pursuit. On the ground, police cruisers joined in with the first train stop Croton Harmon Station.

For the train, this stop became a bypass. The runaway train bolted through there at rapid speed. In the interim, Coast Guard Cutters and other combated ships blanketed the Hudson River but in futility.

While police cruisers armed with SWAT teams lined the streets adjacent to tracks parallel with the Hudson River.

Helicopters soared up above in pursuit of that Amtrak train. Ground transportation with law enforcement

decals rushed to outside along the tracks. In totality,
they couldn't stop it.

23

With the platform at Croton Harmon in the rearview of the train now running away at 75 MPH in 50 MPH zones with sparks flying off those rails. Amtrak authorities feared a collision with a southbound freight train sharing a fork lane and bearing down miles away and, reportedly transporting hazardous chemicals. If they arrived there at the same time that collision could be catastrophic. This cargo train was also toting automobiles, and coming full steam ahead. More so it was speculated, according to authorities, the Amtrak train either had no brakes or that its brake system was tampered with as an excessive amount of brake fluid was discovered where the train was parked at Penn Station.

"We are still hopeful that its brake functions. If it doesn't, we are up the creek!"

Said an Amtrak official.

"We need to stop this train. On this route, we share tracks with the Pacific Coast. We rent from them. They have priority over these tracks."

It became evident according to that train's manifest and later verified by a circling helicopter, there were three couples on that train. Jamie Johnson, onboard that aircraft spotted them inside the dining car.

About this time, the train passed through a shrubbery thick neighborhood. The helicopter rerouted.

Later, they were back. After checking with Amtrak, it was confirmed the three couples onboard all used sleeping cars.

Additionally, they could have gotten stuck onboard in the aftermath of the NYC train service dilemma. Their destination was Newark, New Jersey. Which, was supposed to be the next stop on that train bound for Washington, DC after that NYC layover. The train was headed northbound instead. Now gunning towards Poughkeepsie Station, the next stop on its normal route and about 3 miles away.

The platform was getting crowded. Now yellow-taped-off, onlookers remained persistent. On the southbound tracks, a parked Metro-North train resided. Station officials feared this runaway train, if not able to switch tracks before entering this station could collide into it head-on.

Luckily, it didn't but sped through that station way above its speed limit, leaving sparks in its path. Some of those onlookers applauded. Some held their breath with their hands covering their mouths.

Even so, for law enforcement personnel, and Amtrak officials gathered, all agreed that was a tedious encounter to witness. As they signaled for Monica Tillerson to stop and or slow down. Tillerson, on the other hand, defied their orders. Her hustle was way too much for their halt as that train was gone screeching towards its next station stop, Rhinecliff.

24

The Amtrak interoffice engineer continued with his antics. Pressuring law enforcement to deliver on his behalf.

"What if this train blows up in a residential neighborhood?"

He questioned.

"Is there a bomb, onboard? Who else is on it?"

Asked an upstate New York Sheriff as he raced towards the Poughkeepsie Station followed by a convoy of Sheriff cars.

"Gosh. They look sick to me. If they were to be thrown a rescue net. They possibly lack the strength needed to catch it."

He continued while talking over his radio.

"We need to find a way to derail it before it gets to Albany."

Reports an office engineer at the Albany Station.

"Albany is like our hub. We can switch the tracks here when it comes through. I know there have been talks about catching her alive but at this point, we need to do what's best for Amtrak. Not for this criminal."

He continued.

"Before entering the station there is a steep incline. Why not derail it during that ascent. That way its speed would be minimized."

Said another in-office engineer at the Albany station, pacing in his booth.

"How about crossings?"

He asked an engineer at Penn Station.

"I can't see how we got sucked into this MTA dilemma. This should not have been our war."

He continued.

"We've closed off all the crossings. That's no place to derail a train. Lawsuits will push us out of business."

That engineer at the Albany station, responds.

"First we need to find a way of getting those three couples from the train."

Says the Penn Station engineer.

"Why didn't you guys take them off the train at Penn Station? Why was that door still opened? Who cleaned up?"

Asks the engineer at the Albany Station.

"I don't clean the trains. I just direct them where to go."

He responds.

"So, why don't you direct this one where to go?"

He responds.

The train continues to speed away. Now at three times the speed limit. Civilians crowd the crossings. Some just to see this runaway train engineer - Monica Tillerson. Some to watch a LIVE movie for free. Some to say:

"I was there!"

Some, mainly to be seen in the barrage of Television coverage. Some even brought their kids to see this runaway mega train.

25

Amtrak personnel were ardently thinking ahead. They had not yet gotten out of this NYC debacle and now this? It was severely affecting the company's bottom line.

After Poughkeepsie, they concentrated heavily on bringing this to a halt at Albany if it cleared Rhinecliff.

This stop being their normal change of crew station, a reconnection for trains heading to either Boston or toward Chicago. A stop where the Lakeshore Limited train line normally would split into two halves to now accommodate those separate destination routes. Additionally, this stop facilitated multiple run-off tracks. To facilitate the mechanical service of the trains. To complicate the process. Amtrak authorities were now puzzled. They were not aware if: Monica Tillerson would choose to embark on the Boston route or the Chicago route. If for any reason they were unable to stop this train at Albany.

Even so, while law enforcement in conjunction with Amtrak further expanded their game plan. Information surfaced, Monica Tillerson, was at one point very well connected in Springfield, Massecuites. Envisioning that could be her resolute homecoming, and regrouping with members of her women's movement might complicate catching her. Therefore, the train authorities fortified that Albany to Springfield route. While additional cops camped out in Springfield in anticipation.

That Poughkeepsie stop was now in hindsight. Albany weighed heavily on the minds of authorities even though Rhinecliff was next.

However, still onboard were these three couples. Getting them off this train already proved problematic for those air lifters.

An Albany derailment could be devastating for Amtrak if they in the process took the lives of these senior citizens. Yet, they were determined to stop this train at Albany.

26

It wasn't long before a helicopter manned by NYPD began lowering a net to rescue the three couples from the train. Coming in close, those rescuers focused on the dining car, where those three couples huddled. Rescuers instructed the couples via an amplified audio system to move toward and between cars.

There the net would drop and all they needed to do was to grab on tightly to the net, and they would be rescued.

The couples, excited to detrain. Yet, they expressed their reluctance to take that leap of faith.

Unsure if any of the couples suffered from a heart condition. Their rescuers did not alert them: the train would be no more after Albany as was the plan. They were further instructed to leave their carry-on luggage behind.

"Take nothing with you!"

Was the instruction.

Of course, that didn't sit too well with those elderly women who were still holding on to their pocketbooks and cemented in their ways. One of those women refusing to heed the warning went back and retrieved her carryon.

The net dropped and after multiple tries, the first couple between train cars was airlifted. The one with her carryon absorbed most of the time while the train was railing in the open terrain. Soon it encountered a massive stretch of tall shrubbery.

Attempts were futile as the train also picked up speed towards Albany Station. During this interlude, the two couples argued over who should have gone first in line to be rescued.

Continued rescue attempts by helicopter were curtailed. The train entered the station full speed ahead just like it had done at prior stations in route.

27

Back at MSG, three NYPD snipers creatively descended and landed on that top floor. They swiftly traveled the distance with guns outstretched towards Clifton Reid's assumed direction.

Tension mounts on their part.

On the ground, Hobbs, imaginatively by phone kept Reid busily engaged. Hobbs articulated what was like music to Reid's ear: Reid's ultimate demands.

Hobbs assured Reid that he would get him whatever he wanted at this point. Reassuring these demands would soon be met vice vie the MTA. Even though Hobbs had already lost some credibility with Reid. This Transit Police Officer endowed and stellar in leadership still believed, and was eager for Hobbs to keep pushing that big-thick envelope at the MTA.

Hobbs had walked it back on multiple occasions during this negotiation process. Now it seemed he had sanitized his hands.

Even so, his herky-jerky tactics still irritated Reid who at this point was looking for tranquility in negotiations. Anyway, Hobbs through his brilliance and cunning had Reid's listening ear.

Right when Reid was buying, another helicopter circled the building's perimeter. Tossed to and FRO, Reid felt he had inherited not only an earful but an empty-handed Hobbs. So, he punted. First, he took out the other hostages with multiple shots except for the Elevator Serviceman who was missing in action. Moments prior, Reid heard a sound in the direction of the elevator and sent the elevator serviceman to investigate.

Now peripherally and through his sixth sense, he overheard multiple and varied footsteps coming in his direction. Did that elevator guy bring the dogs out? Reid purposed he was about to find out.

So, he moved behind the cubicles and moved towards their posterior from the other direction. Those three snipers all neared the bloodbath. They access and mobilize in search of the missing Reid. The elevator door closed and reopened. Multiple rounds rained in that direction; one struck the Elevator Serviceman who attempting to recalibrate the seized elevator.

Meanwhile, Reid found cover during that onslaught. He worked his way to the roof aided by a dangling rope which the snipers used to let themselves down. Landing on that top floor, Reid boarded that waiting helicopter and took off oblivious to them all.

They prowled in search of Reid in vain. In the meantime, they immediately notified Hobbs of the status on that top floor.

"He's MIA"

Said the lead sniper.

Alternatively, on the ground level, Hobbs informed: "The elevator is now functional! Who's piloting that helicopter which just headed south?"

There was no answer.

Returning to the roof, the snipers realized their helicopter was gone. They saw it disappear in the distance.

Meanwhile, Jamie Johnson fresh on the scene, joined Hobbs as they board the elevator. Other NYPD officers took the ride also to the top. The door opened and the wounded Elevator Serviceman crawled towards Hobbs and handed him a document. Hobbs folded the paper and placed it inside his breast pocket, and jets to the roof. NYPD officers pacify the Serviceman, bleeding severely.

In the intervening time, another helicopter circles. It then touches down on the MSG landing pad.

28

Hobbs and Johnson swiftly arrived at the MSG landing pad and briskly boarded the copter. It takes off in the same direction which Clifton Reid's traveled.

In the backdrop, NYPD officers and Medics clean up the mess at that MSG top floor.

Hobbs and Johnson receive a conformation from Amtrak officials that the train with Tillerson at the helm would be derailed at the Albany station. That's it! To them, this was great news as they can not only now focus their attention on pursuing Clifton Reid but knowledgeably pursue his partner in crime Monica Tillerson as well.

In their pursuit, the information provided by the FAA claimed Reid's helicopter had disappeared from under their radar.

This covertness frustrated the heck out of the two detectives. More so with Hobbs, who worked tirelessly on structuring a deal with Reid before he fled the hostage scene at MSG.

Yet, Hobbs' helicopter remained airborne; just in case Reid's helicopter resurfaced.

In the meantime, the phone rings inside Reid's attorney's office. Trevor Sparks, Brooklyn's infamous defense attorney picks up.

"Reid, you've been all over the news for shutting down NYC. Are you trying to be a National Hero? I will have to come up against these big boys at SDNY. I don't want to give you any false hope, Reid."

States his attorney Trevor Sparks.

"Screw what I'm trying to do! I need your help."

Asks Reid.

"Why didn't you call earlier? You waited until the ship became waterlogged? So, you need my help? Where the hell are you, Reid? Do I need to escorted by the SWAT team?"

Asks Sparks.

"In the air. You won't need them. Right now, just focus on my family."

Responds Reid.

"I can't help you if you intend to remain vague with your prospective defense attorney. Do you want my service or no?"

Asks Sparks.

"That's why I called, Trevor."

"Where are you? Jamaica? Have you already cleared International Air space? If you are in Jamaica, that's okay. The US could have problem's extraditing you."

States Sparks.

"Trevor, I'm a US citizen, remember? I swore to uphold the constitution."

Says Reid.

"That's right but right now you are not. You sat on this for too long, Clifton. Anyway, go ahead. What's your request?"

Asks Sparks.

"I need you to look out for my wife and kids. While you at it, find out what's going on with Rick Tillerson."

States Reid.

"If I'm hearing you correctly, please don't do an Anthony Bourdain on us or a Jeffrey Epstein. That's not the right approach to this dilemma. Why don't you

just turn yourself in? That way I don't end up in a cross-fire."
 States Sparks.
"Never! I won't. Me, giving in? Says I'm a coward."
Says Reid.
"Why not?"
Asks Sparks.
"I have some unfinished business to undertake."
Says Reid after which he looks himself squarely in the mirror and hangs up the phone.

29

M eanwhile, the train continued speedily on its route towards Albany with the Rhinecliff station in its rearview. The two discombobulated couples onboard became more concerning to authorities. Evident by a Police helicopter trailing overhead and dangling a net. Inside the Amtrak office in Albany, operators are discombobulated. Two trains sit on opposite tracks inside the station.

"We need that northbound track clear!"

Shouts one of the operators.

"I thought we were derailing the runaway before its arrival. I mean between Rhinecliff and Albany."

Says an on the ground station operator.

"You've got to be kidding me! One thing goes wrong and that runaway demolishes the entire station. I'm afraid you are not thinking on your feet. Let's get 449 out of there ASAP."

"You got it!"

Says the Ground Operator.

Moments later, train 449 is hauled away to one of the train yard's reserve tracks to accommodate the runaway derailment after it arrives.

"Station Op, I'm from Railroad safety campaign. How many crossings between Rhinecliff and Albany?"

"The last time I checked there were ten."

"Darn! Ten? The last two were dysfunctional. Luckily, there were no crossers."

"Those remaining eight, run through highly populated residential neighborhoods."

"Darn, this could run into rush hour traffic."

"Not only that. School buses could still be making their drop-offs. It's Monday and now after-school hours are upon us. How are we going to handle this?"

115

Asks the Amtrak Operator.

"Where does that one-lane track ends?"

Asks the Railway Inspector.

"I thought we were dealing with those crossings?"

Asks the Amtrak Operator.

"We are dealing with both probabilities."

Says the Railroad Inspector.

"Right after crossing number six. Do you copy?"

"I'm afraid we've got bad news. There's a freight train headed southbound and loaded with hydrochloric acid. It has priority over that main-line."

Says the Railroad Inspector.

"Where did that tornado originate? Canada? Acid? Did I hear you say acid?"

Asks the Amtrak Operator.

"That's what they are telling me."

"Where is it now?"

Asks the Amtrak Operator.

"South of Albany and north of Rhinecliff."

Replies the rattled Railroad Inspector.

"Holy smokes! Why would the MTA wish this demon on us? For all, we've been to them? These tracks will disintegrate like ashes against the wind. Rhinecliff? Will they both intersect?"

Asks the Amtrak Operator.

"It's your guess."

He continues.

"At the speed, this freight train is coming. There's at least a three-minute passage-chasm."

Says the Railroad inspector.

He continues:

"We are now collaborating with local authorities. We'll need to secure those remaining six railroad crossings as well as hoping these two trains don't ever collide."

"Hope?"

Asks the Amtrak Operator.

"Yes. Hope. You nor I have any way of either stopping or slowing down any of those trains. That freight train is more than a mile long. Unless by the waving of some magic wand. It could cross that fork in two minutes and thirty seconds at its current speed. Unless that runaway train speeds up we'll be in good shape. If not, we are screwed! Let's keep our fingers crossed."

Says the Railroad Inspector.

"I'm tired of crossing my fingers since this all began."

Says the Amtrak Operator.

30

At the next upcoming railroad crossing, multiple vehicles are sidelined due to a dysfunctional signal. A law enforcement officer instructs motorists to remain in their vehicles until this Amtrak runaway crosses. In the meantime, no signal lights or crossing bells alert, any.

Two speeding cars involved in a chase become unstoppable and cross the tracks. They are inevitably demolished. The Amtrak train is slowed slightly in its path.

The community is raveled. Now seen on TV, the Operators at the Albany Station are discombobulated eyeing additional pending danger on this train's route. The news spin unfavorably for the train line. The media is not only spun when and how this train service dilemma all began but when and how it might all end. This normally civil community has by now seen and experienced too much in the last few hours.

Helicopters continue to trail this runaway with Monica Tillerson at the helm. Over some loud audio, Tillerson from their cockpit is warned regarding not only her surrender but the impending danger up ahead per the oncoming freight train. Tillerson remains non-committal. Although seeing those displayed dangers up ahead signs waving at her at that last crossing.

Meanwhile, one helicopter drops a net for those two couples on the train. In multiple succession, they are rescued.

Monica Tillerson hears the horn from the freight train in the distance. She whimpers as the freight train finally bears down approaching the fork up ahead. Her train is doing 85 MPH in a 75 MPH zone. The freight train is doing 90 MPH.

The freight train is now at runaway speed. Its horn crescendo. Albany Operators juggle phone lines wondering if this tornado will clear their train. Both trains are nearing that fork. The freight train's horn crescendo. The Amtrak train's caboose clips the last car of that freight train. Luckily, it only toted a mud bike.

31

With the runaway train just a few miles south of Albany Station. Monica Tillerson's cell phone rings. She IDs the caller. It's a familiar number by that smirk on her face. Monica answers spontaneously.

"Clifton, where the hell are you?"

"I'm up above!"

Reid responds.

"You mean, you are in Heaven already? I'm still down here fighting Satan and his wicked angels."

Tillerson responds.

"No. Look up! I'm in the copter."

Says Reid.

"I've seen so many of them... I can't trust anyone. Even on the inside. Another Insider?"

Says Tillerson.

"You are so jaded."

Responds Reid.

"I'm dropping a net for you to climb up."

"What do I need a net for? I'm not a fish. My name is Monica. Not Robin the fish nor the bird."

Tillerson responds.

"Monica. If you know what I know, you will catch this net and get off that train. It's dangling to your right."

Says Reid authoritatively.

"Cliff, I don't need a net. I'm heading to Springfield, Massachusetts, and I know how to get there. My peeps are waiting for me with a prepared bunker."

Says Tillerson.

"I don't want to treat you like a fish nor a chick. However, you are missing the boat, Tillerson. They are planning to derail the train you are sitting comfortably in. At your next stop, Albany which is a few miles up ahead. You need to get off that death mobile."

Says Reid.

"My destination is Springfield. I have promises to keep."

Responds Tillerson.

"Yeah. But you won't make it."

Says Reid.

"Cliff, I will. That switch at Albany will malfunction. They always do. Remember the 'Unstoppable?'

Says Tillerson.

"You have not been watching the news. If it doesn't that crossing at the Boston/Chicago fork is littered with law enforcement. They are set to derail it manually at that intersection if Albany fails."

Says Reid.

"I don't think they will put themselves in harm's way. Springfield baby!"

Says Tillerson.

"You should have watched the news."

"There is no TV up in here."

Responds Tillerson.

"There are Apps for Cable channels on your smartphone."

Instructs Reid.

"Cliff, you know I've always owned a razor 'a flip' what do you call that, a dumbphone? Well, I still own it. Those smarties are way too expensive for me."

Meanwhile, the net dangles invitingly.

"Stop playing around, Monica. In a few moments, the air above you could be littered with cops in helicopters. Then you won't hear me any longer. Do you know the train you are on has no brakes, and that all its brake fluid leaked out at Penn Station? You want to see your son alive again, don't you? They have been talking bad about you all over the news. Saying 'you might not even be aware you are driving a runaway train.' That means you are dumb. Just like your darn phone. Dumb!"

Says Reid.

"Move that net closer to the front. Closer to the right. Now have it touch the train. Gently now!"

Says Tillerson, after which she climbs out. Grabs it and is airborne.

Onboard, they high-five each other. With not much time to celebrate, the train speeds non-stop through the Albany station. Before it diverted to the run-off tracks. The woman last seen at Penn Station toting her defective luggage waves from the last train car.

Fleeing the area, they notice the derailment and massive explosion while their helicopter speeds away.

32

Reid and Tillerson share hard looks.
"See?"
Asks Reid.
"Why don't you finish you rebuke...See I told you so?"
Asks Tillerson.
"I did. Now we need to clear this airspace and hopefully fly under the radar."

"You mean, they are still after you? By the way, how did you pull all this off?"

"It's not over until it's over, Monica."

"You never told me you knew how to fly?"

Asked Tillerson.

"You've never asked."

Says Reid.

There's significant silence amongst them.

"Life is like a mystery most times. If we knew everything before it happened. Life would be a constant scare."

Says Reid.

"You are right. Life is very uncanny. It is. Never drove an Amtrak train before. They do run faster, smoother and better than those subway trains. Their speed limit is much higher, Cliff. Kind of wished they were as high as those bullet trains in Europe...320 MPH. I would have already arrived in Springfield, Massachusetts. Hang out with my homies. So, how did you pull this off?"

Asks Tillerson.

"Greater is He that is in us than he that is in the world."

Replies Reid.

"So, where are you going, to Jamaica?"

Asks Tillerson.

"My Yard."

Says Reid.

Suddenly, they are tailed by multiple law-enforcement choppers. Inside the lead chopper, Hobbs and Johnson command:

"Reid you need to land this helicopter for your safety."

Says Hobbs over the radio.

"Not a chance!"

Says Reid in response.

"What if they fly to Jamaica?"

Asks Johnson off the record.

"We'll follow them."

Says Hobbs.

"International Airspace?"

Asks Johnson.

"Coke 'Dudas' was extradited from Jamaica. Plus, Reid's a US citizen."

Says Hobbs.

"Never been there."

Says Johnson.

"Jamaica? Nice place. But let us not even entertain that thought. We wind up there they can make our lives a living hell. The US might have to go to war to get us out. Not another Grenada."

"Why? They protect their own?"

Asks Johnson.

"They do. They do…"

Says Hobbs.

"You have no idea what I've done before or is capable of?"

Says Johnson.

"Let's see you jump out and stop their helicopter. Handcuff Reid and Tillerson and bring them on board…That's pretty farfetched, don't you think?"

States Hobbs.

"Don't push me. I'm close to the edge and I just might!" Responds Johnson as she looks down below at the awaiting distance.

33

While Reid's helicopter increases its distance ahead of its pursuers. The fuel gauge first noticed by Reid and then Tillerson is stuck on E. "What do we do now? There are no refueling trucks up here."

States Tillerson.

"Something deep down inside told me I should have driven that train to Springfield."

She continued.

Suddenly, the air is littered with police helicopters in pursuit as they cross over the Staten Island airspace and into Brooklyn. Reid begins to whistle.

"I don't think they are that generous."

Says Tillerson.

"Generous?"

Asks Reid.

"I mean to bring us fuel. Seeing we are one of them."

Says Tillerson.

"We were. Either we descend now while we are still on fumes or we descend later when we can't choose where to land."

Says Reid.

"There's the Canarsie Pier!"

Says Tillerson.

Moments later, the helicopter lands. Bullets scatter in their direction from pursuing helicopters with nowhere to land.

TILLERSON APPROACHES a stud in a parked Mustang.

"Police business! We need to borrow your car.

They, board very quickly.

"I've envisioned this. After shooting those hostages at GCT. Now, this is for real. Buckle up! It's the law in Brooklyn. You should know that."

Says Tillerson, strapped in under the driver's wheel.

Reid complies.

They attempt their getaway via the Belt Parkway.

34

Headed east is traffic-laden. The stolen Mustang with Tillerson at the wheel weaves through crowded lanes, gaining access in its path. NTPD helicopters hover overhead. Back at the pier, several cars clear the parking lot to accommodate landing for Hobbs and Johnson's helicopter. An NYPD officer shows up pronto with a black sedan. They jump in and take off.

The pursuing black sedan replicates those traffic maneuvers. The sign for Pennsylvania Avenue exit looms in dark green with milk-white lettering.

The Mustang exits in runaway mode. The upcoming street sign says Cozine Avenue. Tillerson takes it. The black sedan bears down with a flashing red light on its dashboard. In it, detective Jamie Johnson helms with detective Jonathan Hobbs as a passenger.

From the helicopter up above:

"Mustang just turned left onto Cozine."

"That's a copy!"

Says Johnson.

The Sedan tails playing catchup on this street with very few traffic lights.

The Mustang hits a speedbump and Reid's head almost hits the roof. He's shaken up and stares over at Tillerson with a disciplinary look.

"Do you want to be dropped off at your yard?"

Asks Tillerson.

There's silence.

Suddenly, Reid replies.

"We are in this thing together. That's why I came to get you from that runaway train."

The traffic light changes from yellow to red. Tillerson takes the light speeding up drastically. Reverting to Pennsylvania Ave. Multiple law enforcement cars now join the pursuing convoy. Yet, Tillerson wouldn't let up. Jamie Johnson is close on her tail with Hobbs looking for the perfect aim at the rear tires. He shoots and misses.

Tillerson speeds up and merges onto the Jackie Robinson Parkway, a winding, curvy stretch of roadway. The chase ensues erratically. Signs for the Grand Central Parkway, Whitestone Bridge and Long Island Expressway all beckons.

Tillerson, with Johnson on the Mustang's tail, again has to choose quickly. She takes the Grand Central East.

Familiar with the streets in Queens, Tillerson opts and exit on Union Turnpike and continues on the service roadway. The chase continues with other motorists giving the right-away. In the air, NYPD helicopters are in pursuit.

A roadblock up ahead and close to Jamaica Estates presents a deterrent for Tillerson. Cleverly she makes a detour rerouting to a 360 and back onto the Grand Central Parkway.

It's a trap as law enforcement has now shut down the flow of eastbound traffic on GCP East. Multiple helicopters have taken up residence on the parkway.

Hobbs and Johnson dart out of their sedan armed with doors still ajar.

"Drop your weapons and come out of the car slowly with hands above your head!"

Says Hobbs.

In the backdrop, defense lawyer Trevor Sparks arrives.

"I'm the attorney for the defense!"

He yells.

On the front seat of Sparks' car is Rick Tillerson the son of Monica Tillerson.

Tillerson, with a smirk on her face at the sight of Rick, exits followed by Reid. Cops surround and place them in handcuffs. And confiscates two packages of computer chips from the automobile.

About The Author

John A. Andrews, screenwriter, producer, playwright, director, and author of several books. As an author of almost 50 books in the genre on relationships, personal development, faith-based, and vivid engaging novels. Also, a playwright and screenwriter.

John is sought after as a motivational speaker to address success principles to young adults. He makes an impact in the lives of others because of his passion and commitment to make a difference in his life and the world.

Being a father of three sons propels John even more in his desire to see teens succeed. Andrews, a divorced dad of three sons Jonathan 24, Jefferri 22 and Jamison 19. Andrews was born in the Islands of St. Vincent and the Grenadines. His two eldest sons are also writers and wrote their first two novels while teenagers.

Andrews grew up in a home of five sisters and three brothers. He recounts: "My parents were all about values: work hard, love God and never give up on your dreams."

Self-educated, John developed an interest in music. Although lacking formal education, he later put his knowledge and passion to good use, moonlighting as a disc jockey in New York. This paved the way for further exploration in the world of entertainment. In 1994 John caught the acting bug. Leaving the Big Apple for Hollywood over a decade ago not only put several national TV commercials under his belt but helped him to find his niche. He also appeared in the movie John Q starring Denzel Washington.

His passion for writing started in 2002 when he was denied the rights to a 1970's classic film, which he so badly wanted to remake. In 2007, while etching two of his original screenplays, he published his first book "The 5 Steps to Changing Your Life"

In 2008 he not only published his second book but also wrote 7 additional books that year, and produced the docu-drama based on his second book; *Spread Some Love (Relationships 101)*.

*Currently, he just published book 47
and working on 48, 49 and 50.
With several in the movie and TV pipeline.*

See Imdb: http://www.imdb.com/title/tt0854677/.

FOR MORE ON

BOOKS THAT WILL ENHANCE YOUR LIFE ™

Visit: **A L I**

www.JohnAAndrews.com

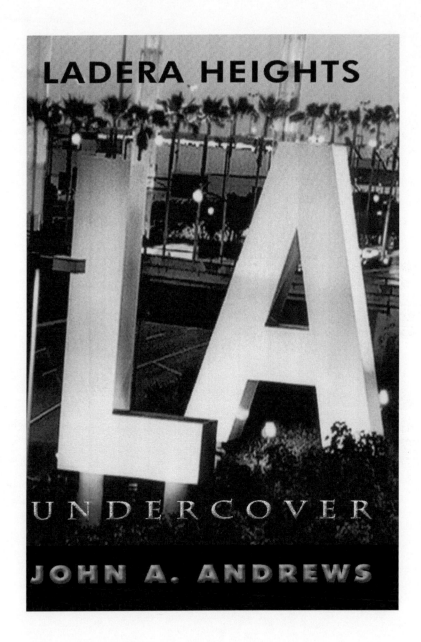

DESIREE O'GARRO

THE LETHAL KID

A TEEN THRILLER

FROM THE CREATORS OF

RUDE BUAY
AGENT O'GARRO
RENEGADE COPS
A SNITCH ON TIME
WHO SHOT THE SHERIFF?
&
*THE MACOS ADVENTURE

#1 INTERNATIONAL BESTSELLING AUTHOR

JOHN A. ANDREWS
&
·JEFFERRI ANDREWS

NEW
RELEASES

NYC ©
NEW YORK CONNIVERS

FROM THE CREATOR OF *WHO SHOT THE SHERIFF?*

JOHN A. ANDREWS

UNTIL DEATH DO US PART

A NOVEL

ONE FOOT IN *NEW YORK UNDERCOVER*
THE OTHER IN *ALFRED HITCHCOCK PRESENTS*

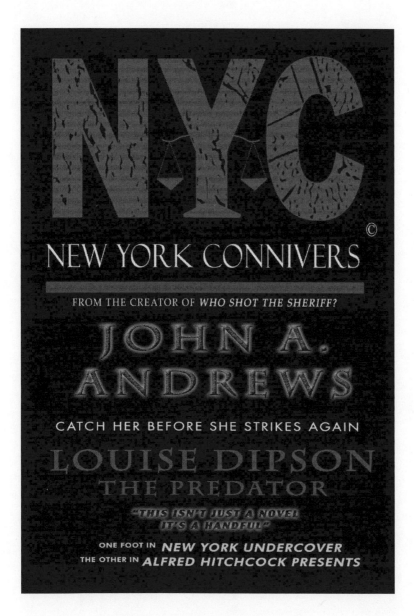

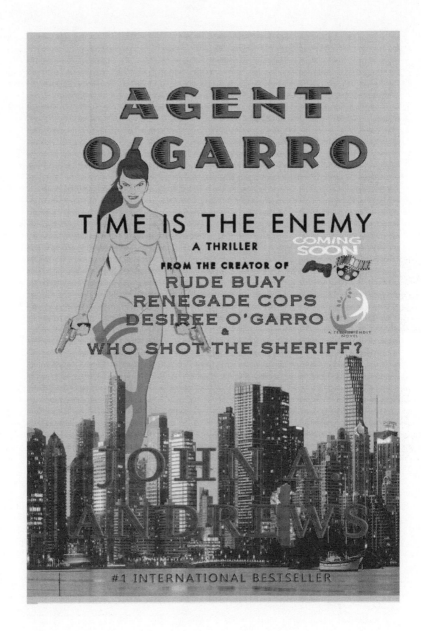

A JOHN ANDREWS FILM

THE JURY

BASED ON
WHO SHOT THE
SHERIFF?

GLOCK 38

WRITTEN BY: JOHN A. ANDREWS PRODUCED BY: PATRICK MCINTIRE,
MICHAEL W. REID, JOHN ANDREWS
EXECUTIVE PRODUCERS: SELENA SMITH & JANIS PHILLIP
DIRECTED BY: JOHN ANDREWS.
AN A L I PICTURES PRODUCTION

<u>OTHER RELEASES</u>

AUTHOR OF THE RUDE BUAY SERIES

JOHN A. ANDREWS
A MEMOIR IN TWO VOLUMES

HOW I RAISED MYSELF

FROM FAILURE TO SUCCESS

IN HOLLYWOOD

How I Wrote 8 Books In One Year

JOHN A. ANDREWS

A
Author of
TOTAL COMMITTMENT
The Mindset Of Champions

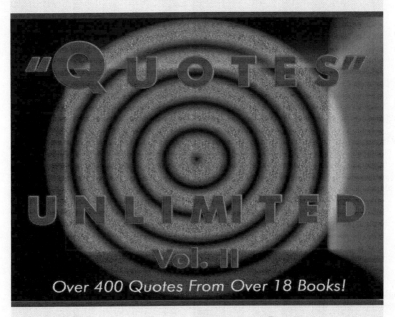

ANDREWS

"QUOTES"

UNLIMITED

Vol. II

Over 400 Quotes From Over 18 Books!

John A. Andrews

National Bestselling Author of

RUDE BUAY ... THE UNSTOPPABLE

DARE TO MAKE A DIFFERENCE

SUCCESS 101

FOR

ADULTS

#1 INTERNATIONAL BESTSELLING AUTHOR

JOHN A. ANDREWS

National Bestselling Author of
Rude Buay ... The Unstoppable

THE 5
STEPS TO
CHANGING
YOUR LIFE
BY: JOHN A. ANDREWS

PRAISE THAT CONNECTS HEAVEN & EARTH⸰

JOHN A. ANDREWS
CREATOR OF:
THE CHURCH ... A HOSPITAAL?
&
THE CHURCH ON FIRE

TOTAL
PRAISE

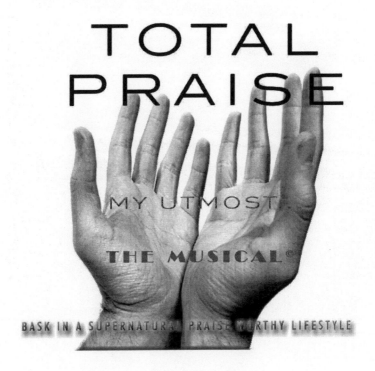

MY UTMOST...

THE MUSICAL©

BASK IN A SUPERNATURAL PRAISEWORTHY LIFESTYLE

COMING ON SUNDAYS
2019 TBA
THAT CONNECTS
PRAISE
HEAVEN & EARTH

THE
CHURCH
ON FIRE
THE MUSICAL®

WRITTEN & DIRECTED BY JOHN A. ANDREWS

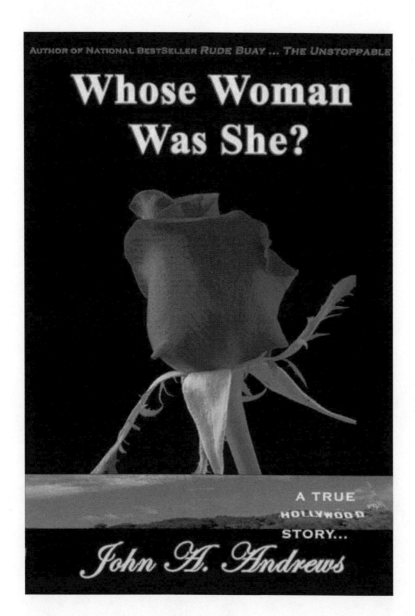

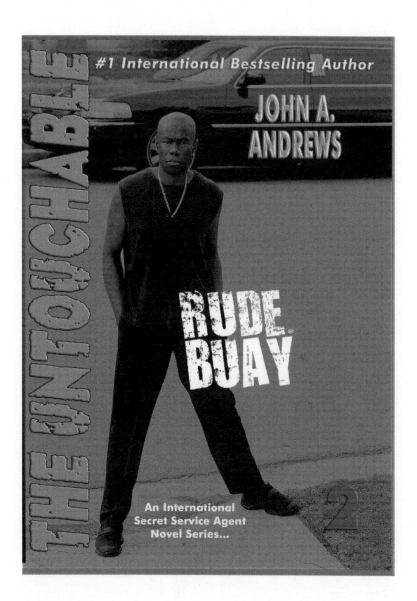

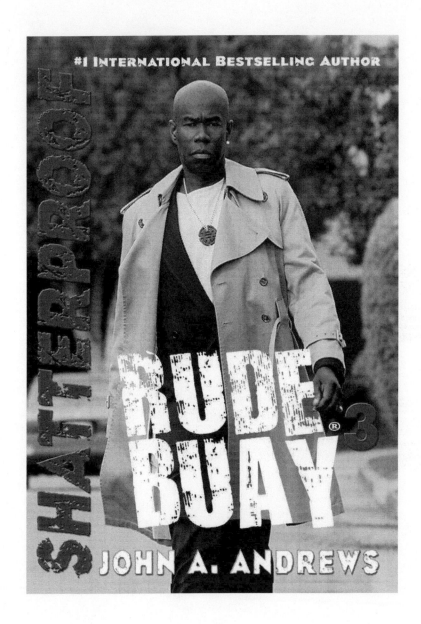

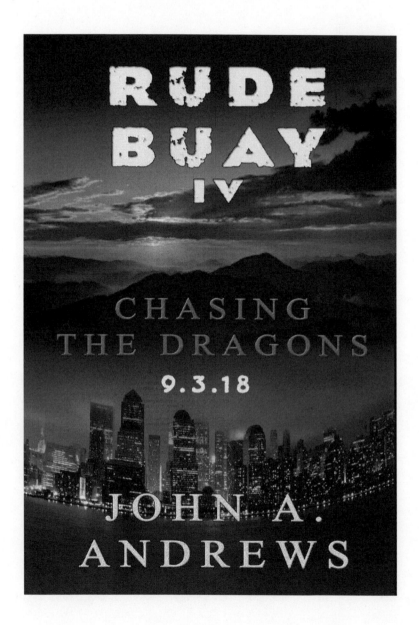

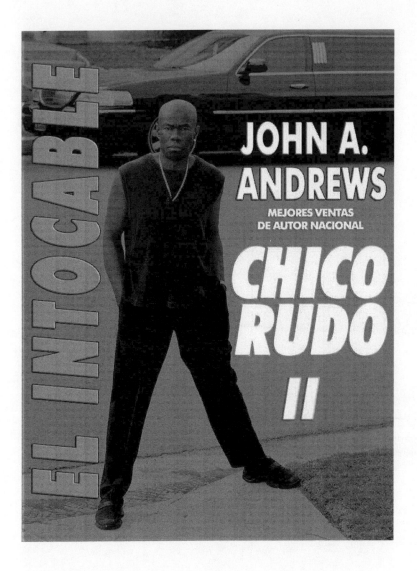

CROSS ATLANTIC FIASCO

BLOOD IS THICKER THAN WATER

JOHN A. ANDREWS

Creator of
The RUDE BUAY Series

~ A Novel ~

WHO SHOT
THE SHERIFF?
The Hustle, The Flow, The Verdict.
COMING SOON.
A 2015 A L I Pictures Production
PICTURES

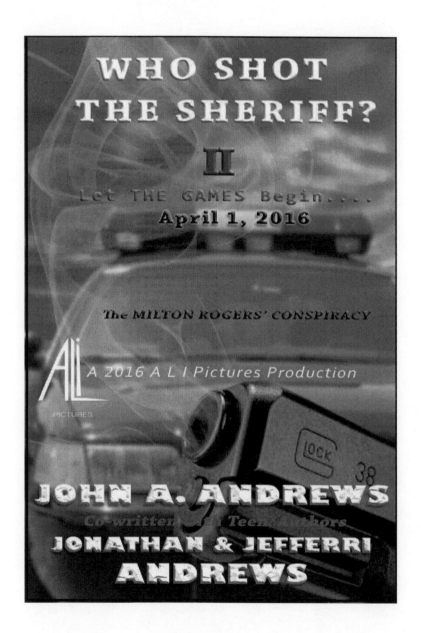

VISIT: WWW.JOHNAANDREWS.COM

UNCANNY PICTURES

Made in the USA
Middletown, DE
31 January 2023

23384758R00109